Published in 2020 by Simply Read Books www.simplyreadbooks.com

Text & Illustrations © 2020 Vanya Nastanlieva

Manufactured in China
Book design by Robin Mitchell Cranfield

10 9 8 7 6 5 4 3 2 1

Library and Archives Canada Cataloguing in Publication

Title: Mo and Beau 2 / Vanya Nastanlieva.

Other titles: Mo and Beau two | Scared [crossed out] scary!

Names: Nastanlieva, Vanya, author, illustrator.

Description: At head of title, the word "scared" is crossed out and replaced by the word "scary!"

Identifiers: Canadiana 20190127732 | ISBN 9781927018972 (hardcover)

Classification: LCC PZ10.3.N23 Mob 2020 | DDC j823/.92—dc23
We gratefully acknowledge for their financial support of our publishing program the Canada Council for the Arts, the BC Arts Council, and the Government of Canada through the Canada Book Fund (CBF).

Vanya Nastanlieva

~~Scared~~ SCARY!

MO and BEAU 2

Simply Read Books

Mo wanted to be

Scary.

Very, very scary.

So he asked Beau
to teach him how.

"All the animals are scared of you. I want to scare them too!" said Mo.

"**You can't do that. You are a little mouse, Mo,**" roared Beau.

"But when
I am on top
of your head
I am even
taller
than you,"
said Mo.

"But you are
still not
scary.

Not at all,"
said Beau.

"You should make your eyes and eyebrows like this!"

"Like **this**?"
asked Mo.

"No, not like that!"

Beau shook his head.

"You should make
your ears like this!"

"Like **this**?"
asked Mo again.

"No,
not like that!"

Beau shook his head again.

"You should

be able to

like this!!!"

roar

"I can

roar!

See!" said Mo

and he squeaked
as loud as he could.

"No, no,
not like that!"

Beau shook his head.

Beau was tired and
bored and he went to
have a rest in his cave.

Mo went

to practice

what he had learnt.

"I can roar.

See!"

"**Yikes!**" squeaked Beau.

"It's just me," said Mo.
"Were you scared, Beau?"

Beau nodded.
"But you are big bear!
You can't be scared,"
said Mo.

"But I was. Even big bears like me can be scared. And little mice like you can be scary," said Beau.

Mo smiled.

And then... he yawned.

Being scary was hard
work.